Robert D Freeburn has a three year teaching qualification from Durham, a degree in English and Drama from Glasgow University, followed by an MLitt in Theatre Studies from Bristol University and a diploma in Public Speaking.

He was a schoolmaster in the UK for many years, including seven years as the first Director of Drama at Eton College, Berkshire, after which he became an assistant principal at The Central School of Speech and Drama in London.

In 1989, with Patsy Rodenburg, he founded The Voice and Speech Centre and, subsequently, RDF Associates Ltd, specialising in corporate communication training and coaching and, in this capacity, worked throughout Europe, in North and South America, and in the Middle and Far East.

After retirement, he began to write short stories, of which these are the first collection to be published.

Dedication

To May, without whose support these stories would not have been written.

Robert D Freeburn

LATE LIFE MUSINGS

AUSTIN MACAULEY PUBLISHERS™

LONDON • CAMBRIDGE • NEW YORK • SHARJAH

A CIP catalogue record for this title is available from the British Library.

ISBN 9781528907712 (Paperback)
ISBN 9781528907729 (Hardback)
ISBN 9781528907736 (E-Book)

www.austinmacauley.com

First Published (2018)
Austin Macauley Publishers Ltd™
25 Canada Square
Canary Wharf
London
E14 5LQ

Table of Contents

Footsteps in the Past

An almost silent city. Anywhere on a tram for six old pence. A concert in a church in the Old Town for six old pence.

So magical and moving. Full of people. Listening. Wrapt in music and shadowed in candle light. Thunderous applause. Such collective joy and appreciation. I don't remember now the programme, but I do remember the release of joy.

Filing slowly out, almost afraid to break the mood and hoping, I suspect, to take it with us. We descended the steps into the almost complete darkness.

A glass of wine in a cellar. The sound of strong words through a megaphone in the square. I couldn't understand, but I sensed danger.

"Will they invade?"

"Of course. That's one of them outside saying so. Russian too."

I began to walk down the hill. A lit window ahead, like a beacon in the darkness. Coloured, crystal glass. Plain lemon glass animals, studded with small droplets of glass. Glass animals in many bright colours. Clear and coloured glasses of all sizes.

Then footsteps. When I stopped, silence. Footsteps. Another lit window. Candles of all sizes and some very tall ones for use in churches. Silence.

I turned around and saw him, almost smelt him as he was standing so close.

"Do you want to sell your pullover?" he said, touching it.
"No."
"Your British currency?"

"No."

A student, perhaps, like myself. Why a Marks and Spencer pullover? Why British currency? I walked on. No footsteps followed.

The embassy insisted I check in every day. I did so and was welcomed.

"I wouldn't go to Hungary. If I were you, I would fly home as planned."

Ever biddable, I agreed. The airport was busy. Once in the international lounge, it was more peaceful. The flight to London was on time.

The international lounge was separated from the remainder of the airport by sheets of plate glass. Beyond the glass were mothers with small brown suitcases and young children. The blackness of the evenings seemed to have entered the airport. Black hats and black coats. No colours. Images moving slowly and without purpose. I felt guilty for enjoying all the space on this side of the glass.

A delay. No reason.

The images through the plate glass seemed frozen in cold, white light. Slowly moving, as if to a tune known by all and providing an imprint in my memory. A painting of acceptance.

The aeroplane was only partly occupied. Students like myself, an American family and some passengers in black. An off-cut of the painting. The city was spread out below as we rose into the sunshine.

"Coffee?"

"Thank you."

So strong and tasty. Fond memories of sitting outside and drinking coffee. Everyone spoke English, so I was never alone. Everyone seemed to enjoy practising their English. Always so courteous and so warm.

"Unfortunately, we must now return to the airport," announced the pilot.

A young American woman stood up and screamed. She was moving in the aisle as the plane banked downwards.

"Oh my God! That's my sick!"

Her vomit streamed down the aisle in a galaxy of colours, blessing those in aisle seats nearby. Commotion. Stewardesses hurrying about calming and cleaning. She was taken back to her seat and silence reigned.

"Only a minor technical fault. We are now continuing our journey to London. A slight delay."

The pilot spoke with what seemed like relief.

My friends in college were curious. *"You should have stayed. Then you could have told us all about it."*

We read about it, debated it, then forgot about it.

I had returned to that shop to buy some glass; a yellow, heart-shaped ashtray, heavy as lead; a purple owl, rich in colour. The owl sits on top of a cupboard, reminding me of that night. Prague, August 1968.

"I would like to inform you that I have made the reservation for you and I will send you the confirmation. Could you please send me your flight details so that I can book transport for you?"

I readily agreed, pleased to be so well looked after by my client's secretary.

My third visit since 1968.

The driver met me beyond customs. I recognised him and he, me. A friendly bear of a man who enjoyed practising his English – separated, with a son of seventeen, a daughter of twenty-two and a girlfriend.

"My son – no trouble. My daughter working in textiles. Only trouble is my wife and my dog. Dog. Operation. Not big, but pissssssss. Expensive. He not piss."

"Yes, expensive." I agreed, having had dogs in the past.

The journey took only twenty minutes at this time of night. A small boutique hotel, where I always stayed and where at least one person on reception recognised or remembered or pretended to remember me. We shook hands courteously. For the first time I was asked for my date of birth.

"A new company policy."

All the other details were there and accurate. I signed the form.

"Would you like to see my credit card?"

"No, we have two on record."

Should I be pleased? Amazed? Disturbed?

Relieved because I could go to my room, telephone my wife, unpack and then return to the foyer for a drink and a cigarette.

"You can still smoke here and in your room. That law hasn't reached Prague yet."

My room was mostly glass, with a 'ghost' chair in front of the window. Glass shelves, glass wardrobe, glass partition, mirror door and opaque glass doors to the shower room and the lavatory. A glass washbowl with apparently no means of preventing the water from pouring away. An espresso machine above the mini-bar and below the television. No need to order coffee for the morning.

Returning to the hotel after a tiring day, I slumped into a chair by a small table in the large foyer.

"Would you like an ashtray?"

"Thank you and a gin and tonic, please."

I begin to relax. I read the newspaper I had brought with me.

"Brie and blackcurrant jelly and the ham salad. Together?"

"No, the Brie and then the salad. May I also have a glass of Czech white wine – what do you recommend?"

"Dry?"

"Yes."

The one he recommended was cool and delicious after two gins and tonics. The food was also delicious – small tasty portions. I had forgotten about the basket of breads, all of which I ate. So much for something light so that I could sleep well.

As usual, I woke several times. One-thirty, three-ten, five o'clock and got up at six-fifteen. My time to think, to plan, to have several cups of coffee and several cigarettes. When I opened the window, the air-conditioning shuddered noisily, so I closed it again. A shower, then shaving with the warm water pouring away and ready for the day ahead.

In 1968, I had stayed in a student hostel, courtesy of the Czech government. I was studying mime on a grant from The Arts Council at the Theatre on the Balustrade. There, I discovered one brand of professionalism. Not until we were leaving were we told that the master worked with his wife and his mistress in the same troupe and they had also worked with us.

Every morning, the three of us from England had to undertake extra – and painful – exercises to remove the stiffness in our spines. How I ached for the first week! As part of the grant, everyone on the course received a bundle of Czech currency on arrival. We ate and drank well and I had enough left over to buy two pieces of Czech glass.

On every occasion after that first visit, I am reminded of Czech courtesy.

"What shall we call you… Mr Hargreaves," my clients asked me.

"Or…"

"John, please."

And Czech precision.

"How long will it take to arrive at the airport?"

"Twelve minutes."

I had time and the energy to walk into the Old Town after supper on my final night in the city. The streets were almost full of people, tourists, locals, and I suspect, many on business, like myself. I had been told that concerts were still held in the church, but on this occasion, it was closed. The poster outside mentioned a concert – Chopin piano concertos.

I found a bar and again was warmly welcomed in English. Lots of different nationalities speaking loudly in small groups. A sense of buoyant good humour pervaded the small space.

Walking back to the hotel, I lost my way twice, so found myself in narrow streets lit only by lights from homes and shops. This time I heard only my footsteps, but I remembered and savoured the past.

Greener Than Grass

I was twenty-two and earnest. Recently qualified as a teacher, I had ambitions. I taught English and Drama and I wanted to be good, very good, in spite of little encouragement at home.

Now, however, I was earning and could save and spend as I wished and I wished to be very good at what I did.

I was also curious; curious to learn, to see, to hear, to listen, to meet and to enjoy the new and the different. So here I was in a cathedral city on a one week course in the summer holidays to do just that. Hard work and long hours, but I chose that. I was going to make the most of it.

A Stage Management course where we supported a 'well-known' director from the West End. I was here to learn and could share with my pupils what I had learned, so I didn't resent sitting up all night with two friends on the course to make long white nails for twelve actors playing witches from the insides of squeezy bottles begged from the kitchens. Two hundred and forty nails to sellotape to twenty-four hands.

Finding twigs and other items to add to strips of different coloured gauze to dress the Four Seasons. Taking copious notes and stage directions during rehearsals, so the 'well-known' director didn't become too tired trying to remember what he had said yesterday. Organising rehearsals for those on the Acting Course – the willing, the eager, the talented and the egos. I chose and I was enjoying all this activity and meeting all these people.

Free time was limited between rehearsals and usually only about an hour. Walking into the city gave access to shops, newspapers and the cathedral. I had been introduced to churches and cathedrals by an aunt and uncle, who kindly allowed me to stay with them during the summers of most of my teenage years and shared their love of the old and ancient with me. Village churches, local churches, remote churches, where a picnic was often enjoyed in the graveyard or the car if the weather was inclement. Encouraged to look high and low, to sit and savour, to read the inscriptions inside and outside and to compare and to remember.

This cathedral I had seen with them and by myself, but I explored again, enjoying the cool within during that very hot summer. Sitting down in a pew to look up at the vaulting, to look at the altar and the stained glass.

"What do you think of it all?" he said in a soft voice, standing beside me. Tall, straight-backed, almost patrician with a bald pate and wearing a black cassock.

"Magnificent!"

"You've been here before?"

"Yes, many times."

"Do you live here?"

"No. I'm only visiting for a week."

"Why only a week?"

"I'm on a Stage Management course at the college. Hard work and fun."

"Have you seen the wall paintings?"

"No."

"Please come with me." The cleric, in long black robes, led me out towards the cloisters, turned left along a dark passage, and then stopped.

"We should really have a torch – but there they are on the wall to your left."

I looked and partly saw pale ochre, pink, black, and white figures, so pale as to be almost invisible. What should I say? I couldn't say they didn't move me, that I wasn't impressed because I didn't really know what I was looking at.

"Are you interested in art? In sculpture?"

"Yes."

"Follow me please."

We walked back along the passage into the cloisters, then out into the heat and the sunshine. Ahead was a pair of ornate black gates and beyond a Queen Anne red brick house. He opened the gate, ushered me through and closed the gate behind him. We walked up the steps into the house. Cool again, thank goodness, because even then I disliked the heat of summer.

A view of the garden at the end of the hall. Into the drawing-room, with another view of the garden.

"Tea?"
"Thank you."
He pressed a bell by the fireplace.
"What do you think of the table?"

A small rectangular table, marked at one end by a neat pile of magazines, in front of the white sofa. Small mosaic squares in a black surround. Nothing unusual, I thought.

"Very interesting."
"Look in the left-hand corner."
I saw a signature I recognised. Lowry.
"A present. A small thank you."
"How generous."

The door opened and a middle-aged woman brought in a tray which she placed on the table. Teapot, two cups and saucers, silver milk jug and sugar basin, with silver tongs and a silver spoon on each saucer.

"Do sit down."
"Thank you."
"Please help yourself."
"Thank you."

He opened a door in the centre of the large window. I had noticed the stone shape on the pedestal – smooth and curved and grey, with an irregular hole.

"Do touch it if you like."

I went down three steps into the garden.

So smooth and cool to the touch.

"The same sculptor made the small maquette on the mantelshelf too."

I looked inwards but couldn't quite see it.

"May I have a closer look?"

"Of course."

I went back into the drawing room.

A small figure in stone, seated in what looked like a chair. The features were there, almost there, and from slightly further back, it gained in detail and stature.

"Another gift?"

"Yes."

I looked around the room at the various paintings whilst I finished my tea.

"Thank you for tea and for showing me so many beautiful pieces of art, but I'm afraid that now I really must go."

"Of course."

We walked into the hall again and towards the doorway and the sunshine.

"Before you go, do look at these."

We entered a smaller room at the front of the house. On the wall between the windows were eight costume designs – bright, almost mobile, and almost alive.

"Ballet Russe costume designs."

"Really? They are exquisite."

"I am glad you like them. Take time, look closely."

I did. So small and yet so detailed. Drawn with such energy and obvious joy. To capture such movement, caught in a moment of time.

"Thank you again – and for tea."

"Not at all. Come again."

"Thank you, I should like to."

We shook hands. The gravel crunched in the heat. I opened the gate and while closing it, noticed he was still in the open doorway. I waved. He waved back – a tall, slim, distinguished man, who seemed pleased to share his treasures with a stranger.

Back to work. I had a list of props for the production. A smooth walking stick. Why smooth? Where were the charity shops? I priced one in a department store – too expensive. Was there a market? I thought so. I eventually found one outside a tiny shop by the railway crossing. Spray snow – something that would look like it when sprayed on wood. Four wooden panels to be hung behind the image of winter.

It would be an interesting effect under blue light – another bright idea for a 'West End' director. Where would I find such a spray? A hardware shop, perhaps. Before going into the city again, I looked inside the shop. In the dark corner were Christmas decorations, probably not from this year or the one before.

"Do you have any spray snow?"

Silence, then movement. Then a hand held out a tall tin, marked *SNOW.*

"Only one? You don't have another?"

Silence, then a slight movement. Then the other hand held out another tall tin.

"Oh, thank you. I'll take both."

Tasks achieved.

Our great treat was the Friday afternoon off before the dress rehearsal the following day, followed by a visit to the local theatre. Three of us walked into the city together. Tea and a sticky bun, sitting outside in the shelter of an old stone wall. We agreed to meet at the theatre at seven o'clock to have a drink before the performance.

Still so hot so, after a short walkabout, I sought the cool of the cathedral again.

"How are you?"

"Oh, very well thank you. Just cooling down a little."

"Still working hard?"

"Yes, but an evening off. We're all going to the theatre this evening to see 'The Cherry Orchard'."

"I haven't seen the production. Perhaps before I book a ticket, you could let me know what you think?"

"Of course."

"Come after the performance if you like. You will also be able to see more of my pictures. It's the day in the month when I move some from the bedrooms to the living rooms. However, I shall leave the Ballet Russe designs for you to look at again."

"Thank you."

"The door will be open."

The door was open.

He sat on the white sofa, casually dressed, with a glass in his hand. The only light in the room was behind the sofa. He rose and moved towards me to shake hands. Before we sat down –

"Do let me show you the pictures in the other rooms."

My knowledge of art was based upon two of my A Levels – Art History and Art Appreciation and a curiosity to know more about pictures through regular visits to galleries and exhibitions. However, I did recognise a small painting by Picasso, a Braque and perhaps a Kandinsky? Then, in the room with ballet costume designs, a landscape by Turner and another by Constable. He obviously had ample financial means and a catholic taste. I paused again in front of the designs.

"You really like these, don't you? Seen anything like them?"

"Such detail? Such vibrancy? A few short brush strokes and they almost dance as if on stage, as if already being worn by the dancers."

"A shrewd observation. Painted to convince the director that that is indeed how they would look on stage – in action."

We returned to the drawing-room.

"Now, do help yourself to a drink from the table and tell me all about the performance."

With a drink in my hand, I joined him at the other end of the sofa. I spoke enthusiastically about the production and responded to his many questions.

"I think I shall book a ticket. Chekov can be rather dreary but, from what you say, the director has allowed the humour to emerge."

A movement of his arm. A touch of his hand.

I rose quickly from the sofa, put my glass on the mantelshelf and left through the open doorway.

When I reached the college, I met two friends on the same course. Relieved to see them, I told them about my brief encounter.

"You should have stayed longer."
"Well, just a little perhaps."
"Think of the picture you could have chosen!"

We laughed and laughed. But once I got into the solitude of my room, I thought more about this encounter. Did I encourage him? No. Did I see it coming? No. Was I surprised? Very. Was I naïve? Yes, very, very.

Years later, I returned to the city with my wife. I was keen to show her the art collection and to see the city again. The collection had been left to the city in his will and now formed the centre of a larger collection. There was a portrait of him in the hall, just to the left of the open doorway.

I looked for the small table with the signature and eventually discovered it covered with out-of-date magazines. So much I did not find.

"Where is the remainder of the collection?"
"Some in store, some had to be sold."
"Why sold?"

"To pay towards the refurbishment of this house. It was a stipulation of the bequest that his collection should be exhibited in the city in a Queen Anne House. A small sculpture and a set of costume designs – so much for so little."

"Hard to believe. Did you know him?"

"I met him many years ago."

We saw what there was of the collection on the ground floor – the landscapes, the Kandinsky, the sculpture from the garden, but not the maquette and not the costume designs.

We spent some time looking around, our eyes caught by so much of interest and dulled by looking at so much.

I had been green, but I had learned. I had learned more about pictures and sculpture. I had learned more about people. I was and am curious still, but I have never been so open and trusting again.

Hong Kong, Hampshire

"And it's your bloody fault we never had children!"

A sharp retort from a sick bed. His wife stood at the bottom of the bed. He was 92. She was 90. Whatever could she do about it then?

My great-uncle was dying of cancer and pain had weakened the solid wall of his reserve. He had been in bed for some months, tended by nurses and his wife. So often he lay in state – embroidered linen pillows, silk cushions, with a table nearby with a bell which he rang frequently. Bed-bound and house-bound. Not what he had hoped for and it showed in his abrupt, abrasive outbursts at anyone and everyone, but mostly himself.

I arrived in time for the cremation. A characterless brick building. Few people and almost no one I knew. My great-aunt was tall, trim, almost upright and white-haired. Her hair turned white in her twenties and it was something that attracted my uncle.

"She made heads turn. So slim and pretty and with white hair. People stared in Hong Kong. So different. They are small and dark. She had such white skin, too."

Today, although it was warm and sunny, she was wearing a red coat and a yellow frock, knitted, of course. It was the first time I had been to a cremation. Soulless and mechanical. As we left the church, we had to pass through the next group of mourners, the black production line. I followed in the wake of my aunt to find the wreaths and flowers. A small collection on the edge of the grass with one circle of shiny, green leaves around white flowers, with a stiff, white card in the centre.

"To Thomas, with much love, Minnie."

The bungalow was as I remembered but this time strangers filled the chairs, the sofa and the corners. So few people and yet they seemed to fill the sitting room. The sun streamed through the windows and highlighted the brass and shone on the polished blackwood. The dust sparkled too but then my aunt never seemed to notice or care. My uncle would have noticed but then he had been in bed for so long.

"We had a maid in Glasgow and two in Hong Kong. My niece sometimes helps here and her husband, of course, tidies the garden. So good to me. Of course your uncle never cared for either of them."

My great-uncle was very cut and dried in his attitude. Liked or disliked. Nothing else. However, I did know why he disliked his wife's relatives.

"Lost all his money after the war. A stupid man. I paid his debts, set him up in a small house. Should have bought one further away."

Persuaded by my aunt, no doubt. In exasperation, he would have agreed, eventually, for peace. When we had tea in the garden in the rattan chairs there would be a man tidying the far borders on occasion. I never remember him joining us. The price he paid. The price my uncle exacted. Small silver spoons clinked on fine china. A cake and scones from the shop nearby, and untidy sandwiches. My aunt never cooked. What they ate in the winter, I had no idea. Food from shops heated in the out-of-date oven? They were both slim and vain, so perhaps what they ate was not important. Or perhaps, as part of the penalty, cooking was in addition to gardening by my aunt's niece.

As a small boy, I was introduced to my wider family. A small hamper would be emptied on to the rug and photographs would fall this way and that. When I was older it became a game of recognition. Simla was easy. Indian servants with one or two white people. The ship's dining-room was easy too. My uncle turning towards the camera. My aunt and uncle going up the gangplank. The foreman holding the candlesticks. These now graced the dining-room table without candles. That room was rarely used. My aunt by a tennis net. A Mah Jong party. Small tables and groups of four in the sunlight. A view from the flat on The Peak. I now have some of these photographs in small white frames. As an only child, they remind me of the past and a larger family.

I was also introduced to the Devil. A red and black china skull sat on a side table just inside the sitting room. My uncle smoked and to amuse – or scare me – he put the end of his cigarette into this skull. Smoke issued from the eye holes and mouth. How I wish I had that too.

When I was a teenager, I began to appreciate more of the furnishings in the bungalow.

Two extra state rooms to bring everything home. Most of it bought from those who left earlier. Facing the front door at the end of the hall was a large china Buddha, a very fat man with very small children climbing over and around him. Above was a picture of Hong Kong harbour at night. The Buddha sat on a custom-made Mah Jong table. The top was divided into four triangles which folded outwards and were covered with green baize. To support these triangles were small brass-ended wooden tapers and in each side below was a small drawer for the smallest pieces – the winnings.

"You should learn to play Mah Jong," he said as I came into the sitting room. There it was, set out on the table. I found it difficult but I appreciated the attention. Later, I was given the game in a small leather box, with a carrying handle, and the four wooden walls.

"It's covered in toffee."

"Your aunt always chewed toffees when we played. Dip the ivory – the ivory slides apart from the bamboo base – in warm water, then wipe and they should be clean again."

24

I never did so. But when I played, some pieces were very sticky and I always smiled and thought of my very slim aunt and her toffees.

In the sitting room tall hand-painted urns; a desk and chair; a tall cabinet with elaborate carvings on the insides of the doors; small, slim tables with removable brass plates; silk embroideries of my uncle and aunt's initials; hand-painted glass curtain pulls; and lots of Chinese silver – spoons, jugs, cigarette boxes and ashtrays and the set of Hong Kong Golf Club spoons, minus one given to me years ago.

"An incomplete set so it will be yours. As an academic you shall have the desk and the chair too – and the candlesticks to place on the dining-room table when you have a home of your own."

I had already been given a silver cigarette box – I also smoked – which I polished because I used it; a bowler hat, which I didn't wear; and his dinner jacket, which didn't fit. I had also been given as a joke a small glass hand-painted curtain pull which I mislaid, much to my eternal chagrin, because I was not usually so careless.

"You've got enough. You don't need any more!"

I don't remember his name. What I do remember is the contempt in the tone of his voice. A small, rotund man who stood so close, I could smell his breath. We had only been introduced after the funeral whilst looking at the flowers.

I took my tea into the garden and sat down in a comfortable rattan chair. Squashed cushions that had faded in the sun so far away. A tidy garden. No weeds, the fruit cages upright and netted, the grass cut and the edges neatly trimmed. Then I remembered the man tidying the borders. My aunt's niece's husband.

The Stupid Man. He never cared for either of them. He never said, but I knew.

My aunt walked slowly down the garden and sat beside me.

"He was such a family man. His family. You have his hands and feet. So fine. Webb feet. When he returned after he saw you in your cot, he told me that. And I laughed. I could only think of ducks. I didn't realise he meant Webb, his mother's maiden name. A haughty woman. Never took to me, so I enjoyed being away from her."

We sat in companionable silence that warm sunny day. My aunt loved warm days.

"He was so brainy. I could never understand why he wanted me. He designed a boat – a small gunboat – and I launched it. I was given this for breaking a bottle of champagne on the bows."

The diamonds twinkled in the sunlight. A cocktail watch. Small and delicate.

"He gave up drinking, you know, when we reached Hong Kong. Too many careers ruined through booze! He drank very little but he never touched alcohol for five years. So strong-willed."

"I had such fun – tennis parties, drinks parties, Mah Jong and my knitting, of course, because it could be cool in the evenings. The races, bowls, golf. He bought me such lovely presents. I do miss the heat even after so many years. I never sweated. He did. He hated it. They wanted him to stay but he'd had enough. He wanted to come back here. So vain. Vanity and sweating don't really go together. And he missed the shops in London – Lobbs, New and Lingwood, his tailor. A haircut and manicure every month. They came here. He would never go there."

The picture of my uncle is still firmly imprinted. Sitting upright in the chair in front of the fire and close to the television. Manicured fingers placed carefully on the arms. Shoes shining. Bow tie in place above a grey wool cardigan, cufflinks just showing. Smiling, but not for everyone. With

26

some he watched television with the volume turned up – deafness. With others, he took his hearing aid out. Female chatter, banished to the sofa by the window or into the garden in summer. Voices sounded.

"How kind of you. Just what I needed, another cup of tea. And lemon. You always remember."

I stood up and kissed my aunt. I shook hands with the stupid man and his wife and excused myself. A long journey and only one good connection.

I never saw my aunt and the bungalow again. I was abroad when she died two years later and didn't hear about her death until after the funeral. She had died from cancer and her niece and her husband had moved in to nurse her.

Several weeks afterwards I received a letter from my aunt's solicitor stating that, by the terms of my uncle's will I had been left some money – which I received – some furniture and some smaller items. However, under the terms of my aunt's will, everything – the bungalow and its contents – were to be held in trust by her niece and her husband and would be released after they were deceased. The furniture has woodworm and must be removed.

I signed the typewritten letter from the solicitor. What I had really wanted were the candlesticks. The spoons were interesting, but the candlesticks meant so much to my uncle.

"They're stealing from the yard. Pilfering too. Drinking and corruption. Too much of it. It must be stopped."

"He would get up in the middle of the night and go to the dockyard to see if the men were working. He checked lists, amounts, tallies, what was delivered. I don't know if it still went on, but he always seemed to be there. The men respected him. So straight and fair. He caught two men, sacked them. Perhaps the others agreed. When we left Hong Kong, the foreman gave him the candlesticks."

"I can't accept these."

"You can, sir. You are no longer in Hong Kong. We made them for you."

The foreman was standing at the top of the gangplank.

"We were on board."

"International waters now."

"Off cuts, bits left on the floor."

"We kept them and there was just enough for these."

"We want you to have them. To remember us all by."

"How could he refuse?

"I remember he took them to our cabin. When I went down later, after we sailed out of the harbour – I could see the flat – he was on his knees surrounded by cotton shirts. He had asked for his trunk to be brought from the hold. He placed the candlesticks between his shirts, padded for safety. The trunk then went back into the hold. When we came back here he placed them in the centre of the dining-table.

"Never allowed candles. The wax would mark them.

"He was so proud of them. The only time I saw him lost for words. Almost emotional. Blackwood and brass. Tall. Too tall for our small table, but there they stood. He wanted you to have them. You seemed to understand their importance to him. He liked that."

One day there had been a knock at the door. A stranger who had noticed the tall urns by the window. He was interested in buying them. The urns were placed on the floor out of sight. Curtains were drawn in the evenings before the lamps were lit. My uncle went out less in fear of burglary.

Ironically, outsiders didn't steal from him. Insiders did so after he died.

Blackwood is too hard. Never gets woodworm. Years later this fact – if fact it was – emerged in a casual conversation with an antique dealer after I had admired a blackwood stand for a pot. So the stupid man got it after all.

I still miss the candlesticks and the desk and chair, but the memories survive. A taste of the Orient in Hampshire and a taste of what it means to envy, to grasp, to manipulate an elderly, ill woman who, for almost seventy years, had been looked after and shielded by a straightforward – and latterly cantankerous – man from the outside world. Forced to rely upon her family, the world entered that carefully decorated

28

and furnished home. How much more had my uncle held back from her. What did he really feel? They always seemed so content with each other.

When my aunt wanted to have a room decorated, the response was always the same.

"Spend your own bloody money!"

At seventy-five, he had a serious operation and so, before going to hospital, he signed over two pensions to my aunt. For over twenty years, the same cry went out.

"Spend your own bloody money!"

She did.

Did he resent that?

He spent on himself until the very end of his life. Created a unique world in which he ruled. Or thought he did.

All I know is that he introduced me to another world and when I went to Hong Kong, it was not such a great surprise. I felt I recognised it. A world apart – in Hampshire.

Marigolds

Grandfather grew vegetables – tomatoes, beans and peas – in long trenches on a base of evil-smelling manure. He also grew fruit – strawberries (in cages to prevent the birds enjoying them), raspberries (on bamboo canes in straight lines), gooseberries, plums and a variety of apples (in the orchard).

Grandmother grew flowers – roses, asters, gladioli, daffodils, narcissi, lilies – and planted crocuses.

Mother had little interest in the garden. My parents were divorced, so we lived with my grandparents in a comfortable house in a large garden.

Sometimes I was encouraged to work with Grandfather in the garden on Saturday mornings. I didn't have his patience, so my tasks were mostly going backwards and forward to the garage for stakes or a spade or seeds or a box of plants. Mid-morning, we would then sit in the glasshouse and drink very milky coffees. Sometimes I was allowed to put the nets over the strawberry cages and, if they were straight, to hammer in nails which were then bent over to secure the netting in place.

One Saturday morning, I was handed a small packet by Grandmother.

"Your grandfather has cleared a narrow strip of ground by the path. You could plant these. They grow quickly. Your own small garden."

A packet of marigold seeds. Bright orange in the picture. Not too tall so wouldn't require bamboos to hold them upright. I used a bamboo to create to narrow trench, dropped the seeds carefully and slowly into it, then scooped up some soil to just cover them and watered them from the heavy metal watering-can in the garage.

Each day, when I returned from school, I examined the ground and soon small, green heads began to appear. A line almost full of growth and promise. When they have grown a little more, they should be lifted and re-planted about four inches apart to allow them to grow fully. That Saturday came and I was given a ruler by Grandfather.

"Take all the seedlings out on to the path. Dig a deeper and wider strip then return the plants to the soil, using the ruler to measure the gaps between plants. Then, gently cover the roots with soil, press them in and water them."

This took some time and some patience and my knees were sore from the concrete path because there were so many plants. Thirty-six plants. When I began to water them I almost drowned them. The wrong rose in the watering-can. No one noticed while I ran to the garage to find the other green rubber rose. Now the water came from the can like a fine shower of very light rain, so I went along the line twice then knelt again to straighten those plants that had been flattened in the first watering.

They did grow and they did bloom – bright orange as promised on the packet. They were admired even by my mother. I was very proud.

My mother has a friend, Polly, with two daughters. Patricia is older than I and Beatrice the same age as I. All three were coming to tea in the garden on Saturday.

The table was set down after lunch in the shade of the lilac tree, on the grass freshly cut by Grandfather that morning. Crisp, straight lines. The chairs were carried from the glasshouse and arranged near the table. I carried out one and set it down, then pulled the arms apart to reveal faded, striped covers. Polished wooden arms. Six chairs with the same colours. A cake had been baked, cheese scones and small cucumber sandwiches, without crusts and lots of pepper.

Grandfather would stay indoors as usual and read the newspaper.

I erected the tent, a present for my birthday in February. The hollow metal stakes were joined together to form a wigwam, then the green waterproof cover was attached. There was a hole in the centre which was slipped over the tops of the stakes and then each stake was lifted slightly out of the ground, slipped through a hole at the base of the material and placed firmly into the ground again. A lot of fiddling went on before all six stakes were in place again, as it was difficult to measure the size of the tent and the space needed to create a smooth wigwam. I was not patient, so some of the stakes were slightly bent as I had forced them into the holes on previous occasions.

"Oh, do it again. It looks lopsided. Take your time. Do try to get it right. Then you and the girls can have tea in it," instructed my grandmother.

We did have tea in it but not in the china cups and saucers. We had mugs and plastic plates.

"Why don't you get your bicycle?"

"Oh, Beatrice would love to ride your bicycle. She now cycles to school. She learned to ride before you, didn't she?"

"Yes, Mummy."

"Beatrice is very ahead in everything."

So I brought my bicycle from the garage. I rode up the path, using the rose arches to support me when the bicycle began to wobble.

"Now, do let Beatrice ride it."

"I won't need support."

"I'm sure you won't, dear."

And she didn't. Up the path, down the path, up the path and down again. This time she continued towards the high wooden gate by the side of the house. On the final stretch the paving stones sloped and so did Beatrice. Into the flowerbeds. On top of the marigolds.

"Oh, darling, are you all right? So unusual for you to fall. Of course, it's a boy's bicycle. That's why. Come and sit down."

I picked my bicycle from the flowerbed and rested it against the pebble-dashed wall. The marigolds were flat on the ground. I began to cry.

"Oh really, John. You can plant some more. No need to cry. He's easily upset sometimes," said my mother.

My first understanding of favouritism.
My first understanding of loss.
I was eight years old.

Not Noticed

"So we meet at last! Do sit down. Coffee?"

His publisher was so loud, so jocular, so forced that he withdrew from her into a chair by the window.

"Now about this interview. Is Monday good for you? In the morning?"

"As I said over the telephone, I have no intention of being interviewed. What I came to discuss is…"

"But, all published writers are interviewed. You don't want to be different, do you?"

If only she knew.

"And so I've arranged this interview, so your readers can know more about you – apart from your name and your age."

Exactly, he thought. They have my stories and that should be enough. Will be enough.

"What I really came for is to discuss the deadline. The next stories will be sent to you in six weeks' time."

"Oh good. We can publish them before Christmas in time to catch the presents market. Could you make it five weeks?"

"Six weeks. And the fee? Ten per cent?"

"Seven."

"Ten per cent."

"I'm very disappointed about the interview," she said, almost sincerely, knowing he would not change his mind. She

had hoped that face-to-face he would be persuaded, but it had been such a waste of time. Telephone from now on.

He rose from the chair, shook hands, went down the narrow stairs and hailed a cab. If the traffic wasn't too heavy, he could catch the earlier train – without encounters.

The quiet carriage was never quiet. Usually there was someone speaking on their mobile phone, but never quietly. On this journey, the woman sitting across the aisle was opening all the packages in her carrier bag – and humming. He attempted to ignore the noise, but the tune was familiar and invaded him. One more stop, then he would be free of her.

When he alighted at the station, the platform was busy with noisy schoolchildren shouting to each other, a large dog barking, doors slamming, and announcements. Incessant noise.

The farther he walked from the station, the more the noise receded. He was so relieved to open his gate and, after checking that the post box was empty, the front door. He closed it quietly and firmly, hung his coat, hat and scarf in the cupboard in the hall and went into the sitting room.

Quiet at last.

He sat down in the armchair.

Such noise. Such clamour.

What he really wanted now was a stiff drink and to read the newspaper.

Why were people so noisy? Everyone seemed to shout, even into those gadgets they were always holding and playing with.

No conversation. No listening. No hearing. Just lots of noise.

He had always disliked noise. Even as a child, the sound of the washing machine intruded upon him. He couldn't read with such a noise, even in the background. At least in summer he could go into the garden. The garden became his world, a world of near silence – apart from that blackbird.

How could such a small animal make so much noise?

He tried to block it out, but to no avail. The harder he tried, the louder it became. He moved away and sat far from the tree. The blackbird followed and was now on the grass near him. He threw a small stone. The bird moved away, but did not fly away. He threw another stone, this time a larger one. The bird flew into the air and landed again nearby. He looked at the bird, which seemed to look back.

The small brown bottle was on the shelf in the shed – the top shelf. He could not reach it. Nearby was a short plank of wood and with that, he eventually moved the bottle to the end of the shelf.

Now he could tap it with the plank and catch it when it fell, if he were careful. If it hit the stone floor, it would break and questions would be asked, accusations made. He tapped the bottle gently. It shook, but did not move. Try again. This time it almost fell. Try again, with a little more force. This time it did fall and he just caught it after dropping the plank.

The bird table was in the middle of the lawn at the back of the house – one of those mass-produced cement imitations with three doves holding the bowl. As common as a garden gnome. On the ledge around the top of the bowl, small pieces of white bread were placed from time to time. The blackbird ate them. The blackbird also drank from the bowl full of crumbs and water. If left alone, it would do so again, and it did.

The garden was now much quieter. He read and read, enjoying the greater peace. As an only child, this was what he really enjoyed without anything or anyone intruding upon him. It was an intrusion, especially when reading, when part of another world. The radio gave the same enjoyment, creating yet another world apart from the everyday. Television was different. Here the world had been spelt out in black and white, and now in colour. No imagination required. No creation allowed of a different world, a world of make believe to be believed, to become part of, to relish, to savour, to escape into alone.

Why was there so much noise?

Everywhere there was noise. People even turned the pages of a book and a newspaper so loudly. Why? Were they punishing the book and the newspaper? If so, why? What harm had either done to them? Why couldn't they turn the pages quietly and with care? No one seemed to be careful and quiet. They were thoughtless and noisy. All of the time. Everyone.

He had learned to be quiet, to disappear. Not noticed. That way, he could do almost as he wished. What he did do would go unnoticed.

The blackbird had not been missed. The bird table rarely seemed to attract birds now. The water became murky. One winter, the bowl cracked and a piece dropped down on to the grass. There it remained for all to see, but no one noticed, so it lay there gathering moss. A relic.

He kept quiet about the bottle too, but he kept it, and it was of use. The baby made so much noise and noise meant attention. So he became even more unnoticed. Little by little, the baby became quieter too. A cry became no more than a gurgle. His mother noticed, screamed and took the baby inside. The gurgle then became quieter too. She never seemed to notice him. How lucky he felt. To be quiet and unnoticed.

It was so peaceful now. He read in the quiet garden and was unnoticed. He read so much that he began to write about what he had read. No one read what he had written, except him. Silently writing and silently reading. He did think he might enter a competition, a local competition in a local newspaper for local people.

He didn't declare his age. He didn't have to and he wrote under a different name. Someone else won – not a very interesting story but obviously popular with the local readers. Perhaps it was all too local. He should look further afield. Other competitions, other newspapers, journals and magazines.

He read quietly in the library. So noisy. He found a desk in a far corner and looked at all the magazines for competitions to enter. He found competitions going on throughout the year. So he quietly wrote and quietly entered all these competitions, using the same name. He sometimes had to declare his age – which he did – and used a box number for replies. One was published in a journal that no one seemed to read. Perhaps no one else entered.

His parents died within a year of each other, his mother more slowly than his father, but within twelve months. Now he could alter the house to suit his own needs and finally resign from his job in the supermarket. He had taken a job there when he left school and managed to avoid promotion. He just went to work, did what he was asked to do, was quiet and conscientious and went home to write in his room.

"You could have done so much better if you had wanted to. You did well at school, but then you vanished. Always reading. Why not go out more? Enjoy yourself."

He did enjoy himself, reading and writing in his spare time. He could have done so much better, been published earlier if he had been left alone. No nagging. No demands. He had to wait longer than he had anticipated, hoped for, to be on his own, but now he was alone.

The house was empty now, so he could write in peace. Double glazing was such a wonderful invention, but triple glazing was even better. Expensive, but worth every penny. The letter box had been replaced by a tin box on the wall by the door and a new door purchased. The newspaper was left on the mat. The dog next door had been noisy before the installation of the triple glazing, but he was silent now. The garden was also quiet. Not silent, but quiet. Quiet enough to read and, in summer, to write. He had learned to be quiet, to be unnoticed and now that was all he knew.

He lived in peace and at peace. The small brown bottle remained, just in case. Would he have to use it again? Possibly. With only a few drops left, he would have to be careful. Careful how and when and why he used it. That bottle had served him well and he was grateful. His readers seemed to be grateful too. For this he was thankful, for their support allowed him to live as he wished. To do as he wished. To be unnoticed in the near silence. To be alone and quiet. To read and write. What a wonderful and fulfilled and fulfilling life he had led.

He placed the whisky and water on the table. No ice – too noisy. He picked up the newspaper carefully folded and placed it in the folder. This folder had been made in plywood with a leather stem and covered in hand-tooled green leather. If he folded the newspaper very firmly – each page between finger and thumb – the pages turned quietly and rested on the wooden frame. In this manner, no noise disturbed his reading and his thoughts.

He swallowed and read with ease. The whisky – not the first, but the third – with the last drop from the bottle dulled his reactions to the news and the disasters at home and abroad. So noisy without and so quiet within. He slowly slumped in the chair. He didn't hear the newspaper in its folder slip noisily to the floor. He was immersed in his own thoughts which carried him away into another world. Perhaps not a world of silence. Perhaps a world of clamour, of noise, of people. People he didn't know and didn't want to know. Or people he had known. Or the brother he never got to know and neither had anyone else.

Who knows?

A blackbird sang in the garden.

Points Failure

"A leg in the air."
 "Was it male or female?"
 "Female. A well-turned ankle. Slim. An expensive black shoe."
 "Anything else?"
 "Not that I remember."

I followed them to their car. Slowly. Was it just an opportunity for them to get out of London? A sunny day in Norfolk.
 "Was she dead?"
 "Yes."
We shook hands. The car door closed, the car reversed and they eased slowly on to the narrow road beyond the gate. I closed the outer door quietly, then the inner door and stood. That had been the most painful experience.

 "Where did you sit?
 Who did you notice?
 Why did you notice them?
 Was it the same afterwards?
 Where were you when the carriage settled on the platform?"

I walked slowly through the house and into the garden. Sitting on the terrace, I watched my wife weeding the border. A warm evening. Peaceful. I thought about what I had said. Had I missed anything? Were my responses truthful or imaginative? Would it really matter?

I had left King's Cross on an earlier than usual train. The sun was shining and I was going home early. A slightly longer weekend. I was looking forward to a cup of tea and a slice of fruit cake from the trolley. It usually came quite soon after departure and it did too on this occasion.

"Is that really my husband? He looks older, greyer. Certainly bowed, perhaps beaten too and looking so different wearing a light blue hospital shirt."

I had been taken to the children's ward and helped on to a bed.
"Will you take your keks off?"
"I haven't had an offer like that for a long time."
She smiled. So did I.
I lay on my side reading the nursery rhyme painted on the wall. The nurse gently probed my thigh. I winced and tried to recall the next line in the rhyme. The injections were like pinpricks.
Three x-rays. The first I accepted, the second I questioned and the third created anxiety. Why? What have they found? Internal bleeding?
The male nurse was not as gentle as his female colleague so, on the final occasion, a large pool of blood spread across the sheet. The bruise on my hip had burst.
"I'm so sorry."
No reaction. Not a word, not a look.
I was taken to a small waiting-room.
Two women faced me. Silence.
"Have you got glass in your knickers?"
Fumbling.
"Yes."
"So have I."
They both looked at me. Silence.
For a moment under their stare, I thought they would come over to look. Unfortunately, they didn't.
Silence.

I was then shown into a smaller room.

"I'm Doctor Caruthers. How do you feel?"

"What I really want is a cigarette. I only want a gin and tonic and a cigarette in my own home."

"I would prefer a whisky myself," said the doctor.

He handed me a bottle.

"It says on the bottle 'not to be taken with alcohol'."

"I would forget about that."

A wheelchair was brought.

I was allowed to go home. Perhaps age, looking more bent than upright, gave me some privileges. It took some time for my wife to push the wheelchair to the car and for me to get into the car. Determination was all it took. I had that in spadesful, and more today.

My wife drove carefully.

"Does it hurt?"

"No," I lied.

I saw very little. I just wanted to be at home with my wife.

There is no lift to the London flat, so the steps outside and inside seemed more in number than I had remembered.

"Another cushion?"

I sat like a Chinese emperor in state – cushions, footstool, gin and tonic and a cigarette, with an ashtray on a small table by the arm of the chair.

"I've made up the spare bed. There's a bowl by the bed."

I had never thought that having the bathroom on the ground floor of the flat would be a problem. I tried to sleep on the other side, the right side, but I am so positively left-handed and left-sided that it was uncomfortable. Then I tried lying on my back, but the pain increased.

Then the painkiller and the gin worked. I did sleep until early morning. Must have a pee. The lamp lit the bowl on the floor. I swung very slowly out of bed, side-stepped the bowl and reached the landing. By grabbing the banister, I could ease my way down the stairs one foot, both feet on each stair. After a long, languorous pee, I almost fell over. My knee hit the side of the bath and my hand hit the tiles. I straightened and turned. The throne was still in the sitting room. Cool and comfortable as I eased into it. First one leg and then the other on to the footstool. Pushing myself into the chair I was more upright, more together, more in control.

"Don't know whether to treat you like a child or an idiot," said my wife in the morning.

"I feel fine," I said.

There was a telephone number to call – the Railway Police.

"I left a small black leather bag on the train."

"What was in it?"

"Dirty laundry mainly – shirts and socks and knickers. Also a Marks and Spencer's bag with new navy blue socks. And a pair of spectacles. Please don't worry if none of these are found. Other people will have lost more important items."

"We did find some rings, and of course, someone always loses a Rolex watch."

Three weeks later I took the train from Norfolk to London. On the way home, I sat in the same seat in the same carriage.

"If you fall off a horse, get on again as soon as possible."

As we approached Potter's Bar Station, the carriage fell silent. I hadn't expected that reaction, which was prolonged as the train moved very slowly. Fortunately, I had more on my mind.

"You have to claim," my wife said emphatically.

"I really don't want to. Let it go."

"But what about those who died? The young mother with two small children, whose husband was killed. If you don't claim, they may suffer. It's the rail company that should suffer – in their pockets."

We didn't need the money. I was alive. I was working again. A little sore at times but that would fade with time.

I consulted a solicitor.

"It could appear later. Many people suffer later in life. Nightmares. Flashbacks. With a claim for post-traumatic stress disorder, there would be a bigger claim. Of course, you would have to be examined by an expert."

She was very persistent, even aggressive. Perhaps that's why I responded so emphatically.

"No. Just claim what I lost, what was damaged – and replacement jacket and trousers from which the blood cannot be removed or the tears invisibly mended. And a new pair of spectacles."

The case was eventually settled and I didn't have to appear as a witness. £2000 and the remainder some months later. Much of it still remains in a separate account towards a new car, when that need arises.

What I miss mostly are my teeth. I had been totally unaware but when I went for a regular check-up, the dentist was amazed by the damage to teeth on the left-hand side of my mouth. Seven teeth were removed eventually so I am now blessed with two denture plates.

The old lived. The young died. Perhaps we had more flesh and fat, so we bounced. The same accident has happened at least twice again at different points on different lines. I no longer travel between Norfolk and London. However, I still travel by train rather than air if at all possible. This is rarely possible but it is still such a pleasant way to travel.

It shouldn't bloody well have happened.

It did. I survived. I still think about the woman who died on the road seated in her car under the platform when a metal bar fell through the sun roof and killed her. I still think about the young woman's leg in the air – dead. But I don't have nightmares or flashbacks – and I'm still in one piece and not dribbling yet, except when asleep.

The Amateur Sleuths

First, Introductions

I am Russell, a pedigree Jack Russell with markings of ginger and black on a pure white coat and with slightly bowed legs. I am well-connected, bred from Jack and Jill, a finalist at Cruft's. I was born in my master's house – large, comfortable and with lots of land to play in with my brother and sister, and looked after by Lady Marjory and Timothy and given to my master after his divorce. I met the ex, only once – handsome, if not beautiful, with a loud voice and short skirts which revealed legs like a Bechstein grand piano – there was one in the drawing room of Lady Marjory's home – and such juicy ankles good enough to nip. A look at my master as she left the flat – just happened to be visiting Angus and thought I'd pop in – a long straight look from him and I sat still. A pity. I thought she deserved a good nip.

My master is Richard Renton, old Etonian, ex-army officer, stockbroker, married Henrietta – Hattie the Harridan – divorced, Conan Doyle/Sherlock Holmes aficionado and now an amateur sleuth. Tall, upright, dark-haired, with a small bald patch, very tidy and organised and we live in some comfort. More rooms than we need – sitting room, dining room, study, kitchen, lavatory and above, by a narrow staircase, three bedrooms and a bathroom – but then, we have always been accustomed to space. When at home, he spends a lot time in the study playing, from what I gather by the noise, are war games. Fortunately, he is kind to me, so regular walks and longer ones at week-ends when we collect wood from the beaches outside the city for the open fire in the sitting room. We both then fall sleep in front of it during the winter.

The Story

This is Edinburgh. Not the New Town, which is a pity. I did expect some style. However, we do live opposite some very large gardens that stretch down to the Waters of Leith. Lovely walks in the mornings and evenings and at mid-day we avoid the children from the nursery. Tempted to snap if one comes too close, but so far have resisted. It's a long climb home after a walk as we live in a double upper flat, top two floors of a five storey Victorian terrace house. A long climb because the front door is on the ground floor, then the staircase of the original house. Neither of our neighbours in the basement flat and the ground and first floor flat have a dog, so I rule the roost. There are two children in the flat below but they avoid me. Well, they do now after I barked every time I saw them and bared my teeth. They all – apart from the children – come to our flat for drinks on occasion. I'm not quite sure what this means as my drink is always water.

"Russell, where are you? Walkies!"

"About time too!"

I mutter, grinding my teeth.

Off the bed, down the stairs, then the fun can begin. He opens the door, then I race down the stairs, barking all of the way. Then more loudly whilst I wait behind the closed front door for the master.

At last. Then the outer door, then waiting on the pavement for any traffic to pass. Then waiting for the gate to the gardens to be opened. Then, once inside, my first pee of the day and off to explore.

Here a smell. There a smell. Ah, here a smell of Gloria, the elderly Pekinese – friendly old girl and her mistress is nice too. Oh dear, Oscar, the old black Labrador lumbering along towards me. He stands far too close so I'll scoot down the bank to the lower path and await my master. I wait and wait for him and the black plastic bag – what a palaver. Plastic bags and special bins.

At last, here comes my master with Gerald, Oscar's elderly carer, deep in conversation. No wonder he took so long.

"A broken window, did you say?"

Gerald elaborated.

"One small pane. No.11. A small hole. Perhaps a stone. Maybe an air pistol. That spoilt thug in No.10. He was always a difficult child – before you moved here – and now at thirteen a poisonous teenager. No parental control. She dotes and he ignores."

"Not such a bad kid," said my master half-heartedly.

"Oh, don't you believe it."

Still I waited. I shall have to bark to remind my master of his duty. There it is. Pick it up and then let's go.

"Well, let's hope it doesn't happen again," my master said, as he extracted the plastic bag from his coat pocket, stooped and scooped up my offering very professionally. *"Or it may become worrying."*

I rubbed my nose against Gerald's faded grey trousers. Always the same trousers, the sagging tweed jacket with sometimes biscuits in the pockets, the torn jumper and those scuffed brown shoes. When looked at together, my master is more elegant, or at least together. Yellow cords, navy pullover, blue checked shirt and suede boots.

Off I went along the path towards the gate in the wall. Lots of smells there too. Such fun and another pee. Then up the path, past the bench, towards the gate almost opposite No.6. Whilst I waited I heard voices. My master and…? Then I saw his head – going slightly bald – and just behind long blond hair. Now who is this?

"And this is Russell."

"What a sweet dog."

If only she knew. Before I knew it, I was being patted – and not so gently.

"Well, now you know you live amongst criminals. Probably one-off. Let's hope so."

At last the gate was opened and while I walked across the road, ready for a snooze, they chatted. I waited by the door. My master eventually said good-bye to the blonde. In through the outside door, then the inside door, and we both slowly climbed the stairs.

At night, I slept in the kitchen but during the day on the bed in the bedroom overlooking the mews. Good view from the generous windowsill and a comfortable bed, with a pillow on which to rest my head. If my master was out in the evenings, I would sometimes have to lie in my basket in the kitchen. If he was late leaving and forgot to close the door then, when I heard the front door close, I would move up here for a very comfortable sleep.

My master worked from home some days and on others in the office in George Street. Walk in the morning, another at lunch-time as we both enjoyed exercise; one in the evening when he came home – I would wait behind the door – and then a final pee before bed. He had been in the army, so enjoyed routines as I did.

The following Thursday, he arrived home a little earlier.

"Walkies, Russell!"

Down the inner stairs, down the outer stairs, pause, out the outer door, pause, across the road, then another pause until the gate was opened. He waited whilst I had a pee, then we both returned to the flat. Food in my bowl, refreshed water bowl, then a drink for my master. We then both watched the news in the sitting room. Shortly he got up, took the glass to the kitchen and went upstairs.

Ah, going out. I lay where I was and contemplated the comfort of the bed and pillow upstairs.

Ah, navy suit, red tie, checked blue shirt and very shiny black shoes. A date, perhaps? Television off, I went to my basket in the kitchen and waited. Keys to the car picked up, hurried walk downstairs and the door closed more loudly than usual. Now for comfort.

I had obviously slept for some time because it was now very dark. Gentle stretch, a yawn or two and…what was that? *Squeak, squeak, squeak, squeak.*

I sat up and listened. *Squeak, squeak* – but not so close.

Fading now. Above – now beyond…now no longer audible. That very fat cat from No.4 going home, perhaps? Or perhaps…

"Russell – walkies."

Oh no, caught again.

"So, I forgot to close you in the kitchen. Come along, it's late."

It was very dark in the gardens. A good long pee on the first level, a fair amount of scuffing on the gravel path, some barking at a shadow for good measure to establish my presence, then back to the gate. There was Gerald speaking to my master.

"What, another broken pane? Surely not."

"Definitely so. No.2 last night. Wasn't there when I took Oscar around the block. Was there this morning. Must be that young thug in No.11. Who else indeed?"

"Have they informed the police?"

"Well, they telephoned and were told that our terrace is part of a regular beat, so we were – in fact – well looked after."

"Perhaps I should maintain a terrace watch. I'm working at home tomorrow and Thursday and the exercise will do Russell good. He's becoming chunky and lazy."

Lazy! Chunky! What do you mean? So I barked to remind him I was there and still waiting to go home to bed again. You should be in bed too, I thought, but didn't bark to tell him so.

So here we are outside by the gate saying Good Night to Gerald and Oscar. I have been told to be quiet and not to bark unless we find the culprit. My master had discussed the plan with me.

"As the first pane was broken in No.11 and the next in No.2, it seems logical that the third one will be towards the end of the terrace, perhaps No.9 or No.14. Entry could therefore be through the wooden gate in the wall at the far end of the first level."

We walk towards that gate and sit on a bench conveniently placed just further down the wall. Time for a pee before I settle down by his feet. Within minutes, a key in the gate. We wait. The gates opens slowly and in comes that unpleasant border terrier, followed very slowly by Mrs Rutherford, who very shortly locks the gate again. I sit still whilst Bobbie smells me.

"What are you doing here at this time of night?"
"Oh, just enjoying the evening."
"I hope you're not going to make a habit of it. I always need to sit here after I walked Bobbie."
"Of course. We will wait until you return, then vacate the bench for you."

Off she trundled while Bobbie wandered around aimlessly. No system, that dog. Some good smells along the upper level. However, each to his own. No one else yet. My master seems content to sit very still waiting for the culprit. So I sit too while my fur becomes cold and damp.

We hear paws and footsteps – and I can see Bobbie approaching.

"Still here?"
"Yes, we're just about to go for another walk. The bench is yours, Mrs Rutherford."
"Thank you. Privilege of age."

So we wander to the next level and wait again. Shortly a key in the gate, then Bobbie barks – well, what he thinks is a bark – and the gate is locked again. We resume our earlier positions, looking, I suspect, rather suspicious or insane. Not a good look.

"No action so far. Let's go. It's midnight. Must be patient."

Thursday night, the same procedure. Sitting still and no barking. This time I make the most of it and have two pees. The second was a bit of a squeeze, but an offering anyway.

The key, the slow opening of the gate and – thank goodness – not Bobbie and Mrs Rutherford. We probably scared them off. The gate is locked again and a tall, slim figure begins to walk along the upper level. No dog, so I wouldn't bark anyway. We sit still. The figure pauses, looks around and waits. My master rises and walks into the flowerbed to avoid the gravel path. I follow. He pauses. I pause. What is happening? The figure is just standing still and looking upwards at the terrace. We move closer. Something is taken from a coat pocket in one hand while the figure bends down, then stands upright again. Pause. We walk a little closer, then a sound like a pistol shot. So much for remaining undercover.

"Damn!"

Says my master. Trodden on a dry twig. Not exactly subtle. The figure turns and sees us in the flowerbed.

"Lost Russell's ball. Determined to find it. His favourite."

How embarrassing. I don't have a ball, so certainly no favourite. Makes me seem stupid.

"Would you like me to help you look?"

"Very kind, but no thank you."

With that, the male figure – deep male voice, but sounds young – walked slowly back towards the gate, opened it and left the gardens.

"Now that's very suspicious, don't you think, Russell? What was he doing?"

Almost as suspicious as us standing in the flowerbed at this time of night. I felt like barking, but didn't. Off home now after another unsuccessful investigation.

However, my master's curiosity was aroused so the following night the same procedure again. This time we changed our location and stood further along the flowerbed behind the trunk of a tree. Bobbie found me and barked. I sat silently.

"Bobbie, here boy! Nothing there, so come here."

Another bark, then obediently he left us alone. I would like to have nipped him but too well-behaved and too well-bred for that. Anyway, he wasn't worth the effort.

Silence.

My master wasn't comfortable, so began to shift from foot to foot. A key in the gate, footsteps on the gravel, then silence again. My master moved around the tree trunk and I moved around the other side. It was the youth again. Footsteps on the gravel path until they stopped very close. Bent down, picked something from the path, stood upright again and took something from his coat pocket.

Ping. Crash. Splinter.

"And what do you think you're doing?"

He turned towards the gate but my master was too quick for him. Grabbed his arm and, in a pincer movement, I dug my teeth into his trouser leg. What a team!

"I was just taking a walk," the youth spluttered.

"Well, let us see what you were looking at."

My master marched him towards the gate opposite our home.

In the darkness I noticed an object on the gravel, caught in the lamplight now. I took it up in my teeth – soft and rubbery and weighted so it bounced against my chest. I too went towards the open gate to find my master and the youth standing in the middle of the road.

"I'm not convinced you were just out for a walk."

"But I was. What else would I be doing?"

"Exactly."

They walked together to No.1, then slowly walked along the terrace, past the broken pane in No.2, past No.11 where the broken pane was covered with cling film.

"I really should be going home. My parents will be back and will wonder where I am."

"Not before we have completed the terrace."

With this, the youth attempted to break the hold of my master. Army grip, so no luck there.

"Ah, at last! Another broken pane, No.24. Good shot from where you stood."

"What do you mean?"

Meanwhile, I had been trundling along behind the pair, bumped into my master, who had stopped rather abruptly, dropped what I was carrying and barked. With that, we all looked down at the pavement.

"Ah, ah. So that's how you did it. This is a small, expensive and lethal catapult. A small stone, a small hole in a pane of glass. Good aim though, from that distance. But why?"

"I didn't do it. It wasn't me."

"Oh then, perhaps it was Russell. After all, he was carrying it."

"I know it couldn't have been your dog."

"Well, it wasn't me," said my master with a cold stare.

The youth stood stock still and looked down at the pavement.

"What's your name and where do you live?" said my master, enjoying issuing instructions.

"Jonathan Ashton. In the terrace beyond the wooden gate. But you won't tell my parents. My father would skin me alive."

"So why did you do it?"

"The truth is I'm in the school's shooting team and I want to be chosen for the next competition. I wanted to improve my aim."

"Oh, so next time it would be with a gun and not a catapult?"

"Oh no, I wouldn't do that. What are you going to do now?"

My master paused and paused and paused.

"Meet us tomorrow night at 9.30 at the bench behind the wooden gate and I will tell you of my decision."

"Give me a hint."

"Tomorrow at 9.30. Now go home."

Clutching the catapult, we also went home.

The following day was uneventful. Walks as usual, lots of sleep on the bed in the afternoon as my master was in his office. As it was going to be a long day, we both dozed after supper.

"Come on, Russell, time for action."

Through the gate, time for a pee – oh, and a new smell – then walking towards the wooden gate. The youth was waiting.

"What have you decided? I didn't sleep last night at all, worrying."

"Good," said my master with emphasis and enthusiasm. Then the ex-army officer entered the fray and the Court Martial began.

"You have committed a crime and should be punished. First, how much pocket money do you receive each week?"

"Nothing. I do a paper round on Saturday and Sunday mornings, then work in Morrison's on the same mornings."

"So how much do you earn? Are you paid weekly or monthly?"

"Weekly. In all I earn £48."

"So, at the end of this week you will put £12 in three envelopes with a typewritten note of guilt and apology. No name, no address. Agreed?"

"I shall have almost nothing to spend on myself."

"Good," said my master again, with emphasis and enthusiasm.

"Secondly, you will keep yourself in preparation for when we need your help."

"What do you mean?"

"Well, I suspect you're not the only teenage potential criminal in the area. Now that we have reformed you – we have, haven't we," – the youth nodded – *"you could assist us.*

Become an amateur sleuth. That's what we are in our spare time. Agreed?"

"Agreed!"

"So how do we contact you?"

"I walk along this terrace every week-day morning at about eight o'clock on my way to school. Would that do?"

"That would do very well," said my master again with emphasis and enthusiasm and again with a long, hard stare which I am certain the youth could feel through the darkness.

For some weeks, we were quietly proud of solving our first case. I had been congratulated, bought two delicious bones and a more comfortable and capacious bed. My master had treated himself to a magnifying glass – I know that because I had to look at my first bone through it – and a pipe with a very long stem. He also showed me a picture of Sherlock Holmes holding both a magnifying glass and a pipe. I wagged my tail in appreciation and barked in agreement that they could be related.

Then we waited for our next investigation. We saw Jonathan on some mornings and practised our cold stares, and waited, and waited. Hattie the Harridan visited again, but only briefly, thank goodness. I expect the whole terrace knew she was about and I went upstairs to escape the noise. We went home for week-ends, which we both enjoyed. I was introduced to a very pretty bitch – pedigree, of course – and did my duty on the terrace while my master, Lady Marjory and Timothy and three others had dinner. On the second week-end, I had no such luck but I did recognise the tall brunette was present again at dinner. Patted and fussed over me while drinks were served and even lifted me into her arms.

"Put him down, Jemima. He's not a lap dog."

"Oh, but he's so small and cuddly, Richard. I'm sure he's enjoying all my attention."

Little did she know, I glared at her. I tried the long, hard stare and eventually I poked her in the ribs with my paw. That shook her so she put me down and not very gently.

As we were leaving on Sunday evening and before I was placed in the car, the following conversation ensued:

"Nice, isn't she? Jemima?" said Lady Marjory.
"Very nice, but not really my type. Once bitten, twice shy, you know."
"Why not invite her to Edinburgh and show her the sights?"
"Perhaps."
"Oh, go on Richard, said Timothy. She's fun."
"Possibly. Well, we must be off."

I was placed in the car behind the dog grill – what an insult – then off we went.

The following evening our second investigation began. My master was out; I was lying on the bed and had had a good long sleep. Stretch, yawn, fart, and then I heard it – *Squeak, Squeak, Squeak, and Squeak.* I looked up. *Squeak, squeak* more softly. I jumped from the bed and moved to the window ledge, and *barked. Barked.* No sound on the flat roof above.

"Russell, walkies!"

I barked again and again and again.

"Oh, come on! Time we went to our beds."

Again I *bark*.

"What is the matter?"

My master says as he almost stumbles into the room. Obviously a good evening. Now I *bark* and look upwards.

"What did you hear?"

At last a sensible response. I wasn't just barking for the sake of it. Not my style and he should know that by now, you would think. Goaded by my barking, he comes to the window, opens it, leans out and looks up and then to each side.

"Nothing there," and with that, he closes the window.

"Now walkies."

Needs must, so off we go as usual. No one along the terrace, no one on the upper level of the gardens so, deed done, we return indoors. I run upstairs again to listen.

"Into the kitchen, Russell."

Not tonight. I want to wait and listen. He joins me briefly, then sensibly goes to bed. I position myself on the window ledge. Not very comfortable, but I have a job to do so I shall stay where I am. I shall sleep tomorrow whilst my master is in his office. I wait and listen. In the distance I hear a light sound, a soft squeak, followed by another. The sounds come closer and closer and now are overhead. *Bark, Bark, Bark, Bark.* There is a pause, then the sounds move away and fade.

"Oh, for heaven's sake. What is the matter with you, Russell?"

I do not move from the ledge and am still looking upwards.

"What did you hear? Someone on the roof? You're imagining it. Who would want to walk along the roofs and especially at this time of night?"

With that, he returns to his bedroom. Amateur sleuth! Some amateur sleuth when he's worked it out and then ignores the evidence I provided for him.

Next morning, a little later than usual because of my master's night out, we proceed downstairs. Gerald and Oscar are returning home from the garden.

"Hear about the break-in?"

"What break in?"

"No.10. I met the mother as she was saying good-bye to the thug and she told me. Climbed in the bathroom window which was slightly open. Clock taken.

"But they live in the top floor of No.10. How did the burglar get up there?" said my master.

I barked and then barked again.

"Oh, be quiet, Russell. Sorry, Gerald, but we must go. Thank you for that news."

Off we toddled to the gardens. A short walk, then home again. Again I ran upstairs to the bedroom at the back, up onto the ledge and barked again.

"Back at lunch-time, Russell."

The door closed.

He's not picking up the signals. He's not thinking – too much whisky last night. Repetition might work with him. I do not bark unnecessarily, so I shall just have to keep repeating myself until it sinks in.

At lunchtime, after a short walk in the gardens, I repeat my performance. No response. He doesn't even come upstairs to see me. I stay where I am and, after giving him some peace, repeat my performance.

"Off to the office, Russell. Back about six o'clock."

Another long sleep to make up for last night. The bed and pillow were even more comfortable this afternoon.

"Walkies, Russell."

Out we go. Quiet along the terrace, except that the thug's mother is parking her car. Attempting to, anyway. When we return she is getting out of the car.

"I really cannot reverse into a space. Never could, so I spend so much time looking for a space to go forwards into. Even then, it has to be a large space. I've been around the block twice and at last the car is parked."

"I think some of our neighbours now have two cars, hence the lack of space. I sympathise," said my master. What I suspect he was really thinking was why buy a car that size anyway – too big for town, especially if you can't park. Buy a Mini instead.

"Did you tell the police about the break-in?"

"They said that there is a regular patrol, but if it happens again, do let them know. And to lock all the windows."

Once inside, I repeated my performance – up the stairs, on to the ledge, looking up and barking. Sounds of cooking from the kitchen. Food in my bowl which almost hits the tiled floor.

"Russell, he says, standing over me. *All that barking. Did you hear someone on the roof last night?"*

At last some recognition, some awareness perhaps that I am also an amateur sleuth. Small, well-bred, beautifully marked and also an amateur sleuth.

Next morning, we go out earlier. There is Jonathan on his way to school. We both practise our long, hard stares.

"We need to meet. Something to discuss."
"I haven't done anything. I really haven't."
"Eight o'clock tonight. We shall expect you."
"I usually have a lot of homework on Wednesday. Could we discuss tomorrow instead?"
"Tonight at eight o'clock."

Long, hard stares – from both of us. Jonathan pauses, decides not to speak back to the ex-army officer, and nods.

The bell rang promptly at eight o'clock. I waited whilst my master pressed the entry 'phone and, presumably on hearing the youth's voice, pressed the button. Footsteps slowly climbed the stairs.

"Will this take long? I have so much homework. And exams coming up."

"Do sit down," my master said as we formed a line into the sitting room. *"Would you like something to drink?"*

"A coke perhaps. Thank you."

When we were all seated, my master began what would sound like a military manoeuvre.

"You committed a crime, Jonathan, and to save your skin, you are now going to help us to solve another crime. There was a break-in at No.10. Did you do it?"

"No! Nooo!"

"Good. Do you have a head for heights?"

"Yes. I'm in the school's mountaineering team."

"Good. The break-in was through an open window on the top floor. Russell heard the intruder walking along the roofs of the terrace, then I heard them too. Your role is to position yourself on the roof with me to capture this person. Possibly dangerous, possibly foolhardy, but possible. What do you think?"

"Shouldn't we just inform the police and let them take charge?"

"Sensible, but not very realistic. So what do you think?"

"Do I have an option?"

"Yes, you can refuse. Then I shall contact the police to tell them about the broken window panes."

"So, no option."

"Good. The first robbery was on Monday night about 10.30. As most people are creatures of habit, we should all meet here again at 9.30. Wear black. We will access the roof from the Velox window in the bathroom. I had the largest one possible installed to provide additional light. The skylight was rather small."

I then barked to receive some acknowledgement of my presence.

"Russell heard the burglar before I did. He will be in the bathroom under the open Velox window. When you bark, Russell, we will know we have company. We shall then form a pincer movement to force the burglar towards the bathroom window. He will fall through into the bathroom and, until we follow, Russell will keep him trapped. I shall also lock the bathroom door to avoid escape. As he falls to the floor, you Russell, will switch on the light by pulling the long cord to do so. You will be on top of a stool from the kitchen to allow you to carry out this tactic. We will practise beforehand, of course."

"What do you think of my plans?"

"Where do we hide on the roof?"

"Each of us will be behind a chimney stack which we can move around, depending upon the direction of the burglar, and so not to be seen."

"What do I tell my parents?"

"What did you say to them this evening?"

"Going out for a walk."

"Not good enough. How about studying for exams with a friend? Do you have a friend?"

"Of course."

"Nearby?"

"Yes."

"Well, that's the perfect excuse, unless you can think of a better one."

"That will do. They'll be so pleased I'm studying at all."

"Remember to wear black. Unless there are any further questions, we meet again on Monday evening at 9.30."

My master showed Jonathan out, then returned and sat down again. I settled down to snooze before my final walk of the day.

"What do you think, Russell? Is he reliable?"

I barked to confirm I believed so.

"Yes, I agree. What a team we shall make, especially when we catch this burglar."

Not if, I thought, but when. Ever the confident ex-army officer.

We had practised pulling the light cord in the bathroom several times. I sat on the stool, grabbed the wooden handle at the end of the cord and pulled. First time nothing happened. Second time the light came on and I fell off the stool. Very embarrassing.

"Perhaps a chair from the dining room would be a better height."

Also more comfortable, I thought, as it had a padded seat. This arrangement was a great success. I stood up, caught the wooden handle in my jaw and pulled. On came the light. Problem solved.

Monday evening arrived soon enough. My master was dressed totally in black with boot polish over his face, ears, neck and hands. The past lives on.

Jonathan arrived promptly in black, clutching a cloth, a tin of black boot polish, a black hat and several books under his arm. Soon they looked like twins. I felt slightly out of it all but grateful that I would not be clambering over the roof.

We went up to the bathroom. I was placed on the chair. My master opened the Velox fully, then both he and Jonathan used the stool to climb on to the roof. I pulled the cord and the light went out. I settled down to wait, and wait I certainly did.

No sounds on the roof. Then a black face appeared in the shadow of the window.

"Russell, why haven't you barked?"

What a silly question. No squeaks, no bark.

"Did you hear anything?"

"No," I barked. Oh, what a waste of time. I pulled the light cord, on came the light – at least my part in the manoeuvre was a success – and soon afterwards Jonathan, then my master, returned to the bathroom.

"Apologies, Jonathan. Apologies, Russell. Let's clean up, go downstairs, have a drink and agree to meet again next Monday."

Once this was all achieved, we went outside with Jonathan.

"Anyway, it was fun. Thank you both. Here's to next week," and off he went home with his books under his arm.

A week later, which passed more slowly and without incident, or another break-in, Monday finally arrived. Same routine – Jonathan arrived promptly as usual at 9.30, all in black, with books under his arm.

"My parents are so pleased I am revising for exams with Peter. His results so far have been better than mine and they hope it could be catching."

Jonathan then finished dressing – black boot polish and woolly hat – and we all went upstairs into the bathroom. This time, Jonathan lifted me on to the chair, very carefully. I gave him a lick in acknowledgement. So unlike me, but after all, we were in the same team and he was now a full member with my master and I.

Once they were on the roof, I turned off the light and settled down to wait. I thought I might have a snooze but that would be unprofessional, so I just lay and waited. Not for long. *Squeak, squeak, squeak, squeak. Squeak, squeak. SQUEAK, SQUEAK* overhead! I sat up, barked, then barked again more loudly. Silence. Then the sounds continued and faded slightly. The sounds returned and seemed to be just by the open window. Then the shadow of a person filled the open space. I sat really still with the wooden knob in my mouth.

Slowly the shadow became smaller and smaller. Then two feet lightly touched the floor. I pulled the cord, the light was on, the burglar was in the bathroom – another all in black – and I created a cacophony of barks. I leapt on to the floor, grabbed a trouser leg and pulled. I was almost kicked off but not quite.

"Stop kicking my dog!"

My master was first down, followed almost immediately by Jonathan, who landed silently.

"So you're the cat burglar." A phrase picked up from a Hitchcock film we watched on Saturday. Not original.

"Well, who are you?"

Long, hard stares. We all stood still. Silence. Then Jonathan, who was standing closest, pulled at the black woolly hat. Blond hair cascaded all over her shoulders. Her! If I had known it was her, I would have bitten her in return for the rough patting she inflicted when we first met.

"I know you. We've met. You live in the terrace. So why this caper?"

"To see if it could be done. Research. Information."

"You sound like a civil servant!" said my master coldly.

"Ideas, then. I'm a writer. Well, I write articles, but I really want to be a crime writer – the next Minette Walters."

"The Ice House," said Jonathan. *"That was a really good story."*

"So you decided to steal from your neighbours and frighten them too?"

"Steal yes, frighten no, and anyway, I returned the clock anonymously the next morning. I just wanted to see if I could do it – if it could be done, as it would fit very nicely into my story. So you must be Richard Renton and this is Russell. (I barked in acknowledgement.) *I'm sorry if I hurt you, but barking dogs scare me."*

"Good," I thought and gave her a long, hard stare.

"So, who are you?"

"Caroline Grey. And the third musketeer?"

"Jonathan Ashton."

"I could ask what the two of you were doing on the roof."

63

"The three of us are amateur sleuths. We caught the person who was responsible for the small holes in the window panes along the terrace."

"Really? Well, whoever did that had a very good aim," Caroline said with respect.

"Thank you."

We all looked at Jonathan, who realised he should not have confessed so readily.

"Air rifle?"

"No, a catapult."

"Ah, another criminal. I am in good company. What crime have your committed, Richard? You, Russell?"

All eyes were now upon me. I thought long and hard about whether to confess to stealing that bone from my brother, or to chewing the leg of the stool in the kitchen.

"We are now all in this together," said my master, once again saying something unoriginal.

"I need help with my story, so all experience is very welcome."

"Both nights I used my mountaineering experience, but that's as far as it goes. Apart from my head for heights."

"I have both too," said Jonathan, bonding even more with the blond.

So sick-making, I almost threw up my supper on the bathroom floor.

"You could all feature in my story. Especially Russell. Such novelty value!"

I began to think I should have bitten her after all. Makes me sound like something from a Christmas cracker.

"So what you're saying is we should forget about your criminal record and, instead, bask in the glory of your story?"

Again, my master gave a long, hard stare.

"Apart from Russell, we are all criminals – or with what would appear to anyone who knows of our exploits – putative criminals. Better to be thought of as amateur sleuths remembered for posterity in print."

"Well, if we were to work together, I know of a crime," said Jonathan. *"In the mews behind this terrace, Mrs Orwell told me about it when I was delivering the newspaper. A garage broken into and a box of antique tools stolen. If you used your binoculars, Richard, you could see the garage from one of the windows."*

"What good news," said Caroline. *"Why not? The first case for the amateur sleuths."*

"Let us plan this manoeuvre," said the ex-army officer. *"Jonathan, you will be the hunter, gatherer of information. Caroline, you will be the note-taker. I will be the organiser and Russell, you will be the secret weapon."*

I barked in acknowledgement. Better a secret weapon than a novelty.

"When do we begin?" said Jonathan.

"You will begin on Saturday during your paper round. Take your time. Spend your time speaking to whoever is up and about. You will then report to Caroline who will collate the information. We will all meet on Saturday evening here to learn from what has been discovered and then plan the way forward."

Amateur Sleuths into Action.

The Mask

The mask sat on top of the bookshelf around the base of an alabaster urn. The black ribbons hung down the side untidily. It had been worn once to a fancy dress ball in Venice.

She didn't need a fake mask but it was colourful and eye-catching. She knew it would attract eyes to her, yet she would remain anonymous. That was what she always hoped for – anonymity. She had been well-known once and once was certainly enough.

In 1984, her father died. Judith was seventeen and away at school. Her mother had died one year earlier, after falling from her horse. Broken neck.

She was known before she arrived at the school, as the accident had been in most papers and mentioned briefly on the local news. She was glad, however, to escape from home, very comfortable though it was and, if her mother had not insisted she stay at home, she would have gone earlier.

"The money could be spent on hobbies and holidays. Think of where we could go. I always wanted to go to Italy but your father would rather stay at home. What about Venice? Think about it and I'll go to the travel agent when I am next in town."

So they went to Venice in the summer. Of all times to go – hot, smelly, full of fat American tourists and students on rail cards. Harry's Bar and Florian's were always full whenever they passed and full of the same people – or so it seemed, when they returned. How long could people sit with empty coffee cups? Always espresso cups too.

The Gritti was comfortable, the food good, but they should have stayed at the Cipriani where it was cool and away from the hordes.

"Too expensive. I'm not made of money."
"I'll spend my own money."
"You will not. That is for Judith."

So her father paid for a week at the Gritti.

They had one more holiday before the accident. Geneva was very pleasant and the Beau Rivage was quiet and comfortable with a wonderful view of the lake. Mother and Daughter were inseparable.

"You are beginning to look more like me. Same nose, same eyes, same hands, and same gestures. Not that frock – we'll clash. Go and change."

They walked around the lake, had coffee on a floating restaurant and then shopped. One as part of the other.

The waiter in the dining-room was so attentive. Hovering. Anticipating. Never wrong. Her mother was irritated, then flattered. He was young. Thick, dark hair, thin body, quietly energetic. He would expect a generous tip at the end of their holiday.

The fall had been unexpected. Her mother had ridden since childhood and looked good on a horse. She dressed carefully and in such good taste. Money well spent – her money.

How did it happen? Was she dead when she was found? So many questions.

So direct. But Judith rarely responded.

"She's so quiet."

All the attention was unwelcome. So unnecessary. She had hoped to be lost amongst all the girls. Just one of the girls.

They had learned not to probe, not to pry, so Judith became one of the girls. Same uniform. Same gossip – films, pop stars, parties. Oh yes, she went to parties.

When her father died, she was sent home. Seventeen and a young woman alone. How sad.

"We should visit. See that she is all right."

Neighbours. Callers. Her uncle and aunt came to stay. But not for long.

"People, like fish, begin to smell after three days."

Her father was right. They did. Quietness tended to irritate some, to intimidate others.

"Perhaps she'll go to Oxford, like her father? Or marry young, like her mother?"

Quietness also seemed a challenge for some. Johnnie called. They had played together as children, known each other for years – or so he seemed to think. They went to local parties together and he always drove her home.

"A drink?"

"Thank you."

One night he kissed her. She let him do so. She closed the door after he had driven down the avenue.

Silence.

She sat in the drawing-room and looked at the darkness outside. No need to ever draw curtains. No one nearby.

Judith did not go to Oxford. She stayed at home. With daily help, she could manage the house herself. And enjoyed doing so.

She didn't ride, so the paddock was let to a neighbouring farmer. She didn't paint, so her mother's studio became a small sitting room.

But she did go to parties.

Perhaps friends of her parents felt sorry for her. Perhaps not, but they invited her and Johnnie was very attentive.

The house was improved. The man who had worked for her parents now worked for her and found other men to assist in the refurbishment. While they knocked down walls, the garden became a sanctuary. A perimeter hedge was planted. It wouldn't take too long to grow and beech would form a wind break. New borders were dug and planted. Stone paths were laid. Learning to drive had been necessary and now she enjoyed visiting garden centres in the mornings – never anyone about except the staff, so she could ask her questions. An occupation and a hobby.

"The French doors are a great improvement. And two sets."

"So much light. It was always rather dull before."

Johnnie took his drink on to the terrace.

"A good size. You'll be able to have lots of summer parties here."

So she had a party there.

Curiosity drove people to accept.

"How pretty she has become. Not so mousey. Almost as pretty as her mother."

"Still quiet, though. You never know what she's thinking."

They saw. They went home.

The cards had stated clearly – Drinks 6.30–8.30. Dress informal.

The house was explored, the garden wandered through.

They had seen what they wanted to see, and departed.

Invitations followed. She drove herself or, when very insistent, she allowed Johnnie to collect her and they went together. He talked about Cambridge and what he would do when he came down.

"An auction house, I think. Something to do with paintings."

"Why? You read English."

"I know, but I don't want to teach or be an academic. And I like pictures."

"But you don't know anything about them."

His father had a friend who was a director of an auction house so he worked there that summer. Then at Christmas and Easter too.

"How about coming to Florence with me in the summer?"

"Whatever for?"

"Pictures."

"I know nothing about them."

"You will after three weeks in Florence.

Two weeks was long enough. Hot, full of noisy tourists, long queues to all the galleries, every view of the Arno hidden by so many people. Except early morning, so Judith rose early and explored on her own.

"Why didn't you ask me?"
"You hate the mornings. You said so."
"But I would have come with you."
"I know."
"So why didn't you ask me?"
"I really enjoyed it alone."
"But I thought you enjoyed my company?"
"Sometimes. Don't let's argue. You'll be late for the lecture."

So off he went. And she collected her picture – View of the River Arno. For the small sitting room.

On the way back to the pension, she found a shop window full of masks. She couldn't resist going inside. White, black, coloured, sequined, full face, eyes, small and large. The man appeared and watched. With time, she found exactly what she wanted. Green, red and gold that shone and glittered in the sunlight through the window.

Johnnie was like a faithful dog, a happy Labrador. He walked with Judith mostly where she wanted to go but she did indulge him too. Pictures were found in obscure corners of obscure churches. In that way, she saw more of the city and they always stopped in a small square to have coffee, then lunch, and then ice-cream in the afternoon.

Those were the days when Johnnie did not have lectures or talks or a private visit to a gallery or museum. He enjoyed those days. Judith enjoyed when she could wander at will without having to listen or respond to chatter. However, Johnnie was becoming quieter. Sometimes they even sat over dinner in companionable silence, watching and hearing those at nearby tables and those walking past.

This, she enjoyed and, at last, he seemed to accept.

On her return other pictures had to be moved in the small sitting room to allow *View of the River Arno* to catch the light. One evening, Johnnie arrived for a drink to find pictures, drawings and some prints resting against a wall in the hall.

"I'd like you to sell these for me. Then I shall buy others. Hopefully, more scenes of Florence too. Perhaps I should go to auctions myself."

"I'm very happy to buy for you. I think I know what you would like. Tell me where you wish to hang them. That would help too."

A presumption. How could he possibly know what she would like? Presumption.

The gaps on the walls were filled. Rooms were re-decorated in softer hues as backgrounds to these new paintings.

Johnnie was useful in knowing what and when and where a picture was coming up for sale. He couldn't always go with her and anyway he was always choosing for himself. Judith began to know what she liked and began to know where to go and to whom. Viewings in three London auction houses and two local ones and then she attended the auctions. She bought and sold but was never extravagant.

"You really should have an alarm, you know."

She did know and had one installed, a rather complicated one with links inside and outside. Inside her bedroom, the small sitting room and the drawing room. She refused to have grills – so ugly – but there was a small mat in front of each French window and in the hall and in the kitchen.

Judith gave another summer party with the same rules – and her guests obeyed. Curiosity drove again. Paintings were admired, the sun shone and two glasses were dropped on the terrace. Johnnie was perhaps not such a good barman. Too much gin in the Pimms. Perhaps she should employ someone to do it next year. That would be easier.

71

They were often invited, together or separately, to the same dinner parties, but now she often drove herself. The Labrador would still wag his tail when they met or when she showed him a new picture or when she allowed him to drive her to a local auction or a dinner party.

"We make a good team."
"Do you think so?"
"Yes. Perhaps we could go into business together?"
"Doing what?"
"Pictures. Buying and selling pictures."
"I do it for pleasure. It gets me out and about. I know the dealers and the auctioneers. Why would I want to make it a business?"
"Fun – and money."
"I don't need any more money."
"Perhaps I do."

Perhaps he wasn't so good after all. Perhaps he was simply being kept on at the auction house because of the family connection.

After gardening one autumn afternoon, when the sun was still warm, Judith sat on the bench in the coppice and admired the view. The hard work had paid off and it was now an oasis of calm and colour. The nights were getting longer and soon the cold would arrive and she would be driven indoors.

Perhaps it would be interesting to buy and sell pictures from home.

Judith turned and looked at the house. Not very large but quite imposing. She walked slowly up the path towards the front. A long avenue, enough gravel on which to park three cars – dealers always seemed to have a Volvo or Mercedes estate.

"But do I want to sell to the trade?" she mused.

An impressive hall, tiled, with pictures not for sale. To be admired. The double doors into the drawing room, now a very light room. She switched on all the lamps, enough to see all the pictures. Perhaps only in the day-time?

72

"Do I really wish to have unknown visitors in the evening?"

The study led off the drawing room. Another well-lit room with pictures. Perhaps more smaller ones there too.

She then heard footsteps in the hall. He had taken to dropping in on the way to home from the station.

"Where are you? It's Johnnie."
Who else?
"In the study."
"Oh, you've been gardening."
"Yes. It will soon be too cold to do so. Would you like a drink?"
"Please."
She walked to the table in the drawing room, then remembered the ice.

"I'll just fetch the ice."
"I'll do it."
"No. I won't be a moment."

Johnnie fell into the armchair by the unlit fire – his usual chair. Judith returned with the ice.

"A good day?"
"Not bad. Money's tight I think, though we have been asked to sell a collection of pictures. They are hard up too. I'm going to visit on Thursday.
If any good, you may wish to see them. I'll let you know."
She sank into the sofa.
"I was thinking about what you said. I might like to sell paintings – here."
"Too intrusive, Judith. You'd hate it. Strangers entering your home. Muddy shoes on the white carpet. We could rent somewhere – perhaps in town."
"I quite like the idea of doing it here. Certain days, certain times.
Perhaps even certain people."

The ice clinked in his glass. He was irritated.

"I really don't think it's a good idea."

He went on speaking – to himself.

Judith remembered that some of her parents' pictures were in the smallest bedroom. She could sell those first. Some quite well-known artists, some no longer seen in sales, so perhaps there were collectors. Worth trying, perhaps.

"Judith. Judith, what do you think?"

"I'm sorry. I was thinking about the garden."

"But, if I lived here with you, we could run the business together. Why don't we marry, then it would be our business."

"With my money."

Judith rose and Johnnie followed. They walked into the hall.

"A good space for more paintings."

"But these are not for sale. I enjoy each of them too much."

"A business, Judith."

She went on to the gravel and Johnnie followed. He tried to kiss her but she walked towards the garden path and waved good-bye without turning. She heard the car moving over the gravel. One honk of the horn, as usual.

"My money. My house. My pictures. Well then, marriage…on my terms. Why not?"

Johnnie did have his uses – and he was quite decorative.

Another small party on the terrace – after a quiet wedding.

"They've known each other since childhood."

"Almost as lovely as her mother."

"So well suited, don't you think?"

"But when you think of what she does!"

"Oh well, she'll have to give it up when there are babies."

"Quite right too."

"Such a good-looking couple. And all that money too."

"Off to Venice. To buy more pictures, no doubt."
"So many now."

That's when the mask was worn.

A fancy dress ball in a palace on the Grand Canal. They stayed at the Cipriani in separate rooms and Judith introduced him to the corners of the city not ventured into by many tourists. She bought a picture – Venice Across the Lagoon – for the small sitting room. Johnnie was quite good company but she mostly enjoyed the time spent alone.

At home, her way of life continued uninterrupted, except for a chosen dealer or buyer within strict times on certain days. She priced the pictures and Johnnie met these people and occasionally sold a picture. He – also occasionally – made a visit to town and the auction house, always returning in time for a drink at 6.30. After supper, Judith retired to the small sitting room and Johnnie arranged visits or watched television in the study. She was pleased he did all the meeting, greeting and selling and he never went below her discount.

Generally, he acquired the asking price. Occasionally, they went to the auction house together – early train, coffee, browse, choose – and afterwards, Judith would have lunch and shop. Meet at the station and then the early evening train home in time for drinks and before the commuters.

They always worked the saleroom separately, then met, agreed her terms – and then Johnnie would place the bids. One afternoon, after a light lunch, Judith had a second thought about a picture and returned to the saleroom. The traffic was surprisingly heavy that afternoon, so she had to stand for some time on the pavement opposite. Johnnie was just leaving. He turned, waved, came down the steps and hurried along the pavement. Eventually there was a gap in the traffic. Inside, the saleroom was empty apart from a young man in an apron. Judith found the picture, looked again, stood back, looked again, paused and then decided to withdraw her bid. The young man commended her decision, which she ignored.

As Judith walked down the saleroom and reached the door, she turned. He was still watching her as she knew he would. He knew about her and now she knew about Johnnie.

"No babies yet. Such a pity."
"She's not getting any younger, you know."
"Judith's still so quiet but we invite her because she's so pretty – and such a good listener. Men adore her."

On occasion, she noticed the lamp light in the sitting room catching the glitter on the mask. Johnnie had worn a mask to the ball in Venice too, but had left his behind. He had no need of an artificial mask. No, each knew about the other. Their masks were firmly in place. What surprised Judith was that Johnnie was good at it, as she was. She now gave him more credit for keeping it in place for so long. And so it would continue.

Leaving the small sitting room, she paused on the landing. The television was on. She walked slowly to her bedroom and quietly closed the door.

No longer have any need to switch on the alarm. So well-suited indeed.

Unsaid

He ran as fast as he could, with nothing in his hands. When he reached the gate, he paused briefly and looked back. No one. He walked along the side of the road, hidden in shadow, from the treed bank into any oncoming traffic. Cars were rare at this time of day. Crossing the road, he walked towards the disused railway station and through the tunnel that had allowed access from one platform to the other. The tunnel was dark and dank with refuse. Emerging into the sunshine again, he walked slowly towards the village.

A spinster lived alone in that house built by her parents. Where the chickens had run were now two identical bungalows, lived in by sisters and their husbands. The annual ground rent was £25 – high in those days. All five worked, so he had expected an empty house. He had chosen it because he knew she worked in the city, a person of regular habits. A high privet hedge separated the bungalows from the gravel path and the garden, while another hedge hid the house on the other side. Did he enter from the field behind? He could then have come through the long grass – scythed only once a year – to the back door, unheard and unseen. Did he know the house? Did he know the spinster?

The house resembled a large doll's house, set squarely in the centre of a large garden. A traditional design – drawing room on the left, dining room on the right, breakfast room, morning room, kitchen and pantry. Built in the 1930s to a Victorian design. A sign of respectability and limited funds with a quest for privacy. In winter, the fires were lit in strict rotation to air and warm the rooms, beginning with the dining room. At Christmas, the drawing room and, in the spring, the morning room until the sun warmed it naturally. Only one bedroom was occupied without a fire in the grate.

The spinster worked in a printing company as a director after money had been invested. What tasks were undertaken to justify this role were unknown. However, arrival and departure times remained constant except on rare occasions. This was one of those rare occasions. For whatever reason, the spinster was not at work. This he had not expected.

He had been jobless for seven weeks. He also lived alone taking odd jobs when he could – gardening, carpentry, and painting. He was known around the village but mostly kept himself to himself. A quiet man, tall and neat and tidy. His cottage was in a row of three, white-washed with small tidy gardens. Rented, not owned, so the rent always had to be paid and on time. The widow, whose garden he had tended, had died and her son and daughter-in-law, who moved into the house did not need him, or couldn't afford him. He had sanded and oiled the garden bench for them, which had been collected and paid for, less than originally agreed. But he didn't argue. Cash was cash.

He went for long walks, beginning in the early morning before his neighbours were about. He sometimes passed the bus stop by the disused railway station when there was a queue. People of regular habits too. Theirs enforced, his almost by choice. The man reading the paper, the children going to their schools, the woman in tweeds, the girl in pale blue, the elderly man standing and gazing backwards to see the bus turning the corner, then looking at his watch. On warm days such as this, he sometimes sat on the wall across the road to watch the bus arrive. There was sometimes a young man running along the pavement and sometimes the driver would wait. When the bus drove off, the young man would sometimes shout and sometimes just stop and stare as it turned the next corner. He occasionally glanced across the road, knowing he had been observed. He never spoke.

He was sometimes sitting on the wall in the evening when the bus returned some of those he had seen in the morning. Once, he was walking down the hill towards the old railway station when the girl – this time in yellow – the young man and the woman in tweeds were going home. He walked in the road to avoid them. They were in a hurry and he was not. He heard a gate close. The woman in tweeds had walked more slowly than the others so perhaps it was she who closed the gate.

He knew the spinster was a creature of habit. He closed the gate quietly and walked towards the house. Past the tended borders, past the gap in the hedge beside the bungalows, past the house and up the path to the door at the back. It wasn't locked but then not everyone locked their doors. It opened quietly and he was in the kitchen. She came down the step at that moment – and he ran. The reaction was immediate.

The spinster didn't know the man who ran away. He seemed so scared. She stood there shocked at the surprise. The sun caught a long shard of glass held between her hands. Not so shocked as he was. She had been holding a cut glass bowl of dying flowers and, in her surprise, the bowl had cracked, broken and so she held a long piece of glass. No wonder he ran away. She placed the glass on the shelf nearby then stooped to collect the pieces and the flowers. The floor was wet, so she threw a cloth down and moved it backwards and forwards with her right foot to remove the liquid. Then she returned to the morning room for a cigarette.

Nothing said.